How Alligators Got Rough Skin

Lynette Comissiong

Illustrations by
Rachel Parker

MACMILLAN
CARIBBEAN

Long, long ago, alligators had smooth, shiny skin. When they came up out of the water to lie on the river bank in the morning sun, their skin glistened like emeralds. They swished their tails from left to right and cocked their snouts in the air.

They hardly ever spoke to any land creatures. They snorted and grumped and bellowed and humped and turned away whenever any land creatures passed by.

Pa Alligator, Ma Alligator and their six children, who lived near the village of Balandra, were just like that. When they came out of the water to lie on the river bank in the morning sun, their skin glistened like emeralds and their eyes twinkled like raindrops when the sunlight shone on them.

Pa Alligator and his family had all the food that they could eat. They ate small fish and shell-fish and bugs and frogs and muskrats and gnats and dragonflies and anything that flew by. They hardly ever spoke to land creatures. They closed their eyes and turned away whenever any land creatures passed by.

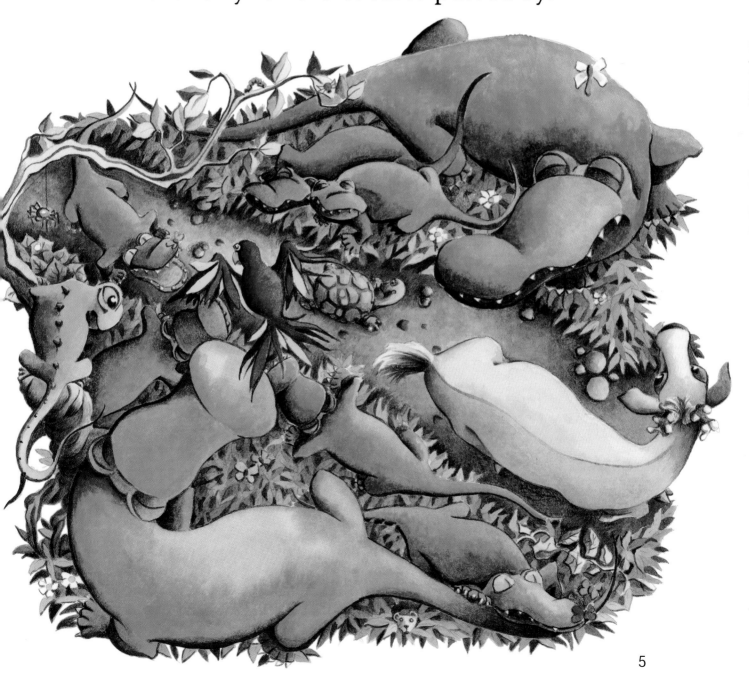

And so it was until one hot day in July when Mr Monkey came looping by and saw Pa Alligator, Ma Alligator and their six children soaking up the mid-day sun.

Just as Pa Alligator and his family didn't like to mix with land creatures, Mr Monkey didn't much care for alligators. But Mr Monkey loved to talk and he just couldn't keep his mouth shut.

'Hello, Pa Alligator, how are you and your family?' he called out.

At first, Pa Alligator didn't answer. Then he said in a gruff voice, 'Can't you see? We are just fine, Mr Monkey. Look how our skin is clean and shiny. What about you? Look how you're always sweating and picking your fur!'

Mr Monkey was really vexed. 'Who Pa Alligator think he is! That serve me right for getting into conversation with that smooth skin snooty alligator,' he thought. But Mr Monkey didn't want to have any argument with Pa Alligator, so he swallowed his pride and just said, 'Maybe so, maybe so, but we're seeing trouble, you know!'

'Trouble?' Pa Alligator looked puzzled. 'Who is trouble?'

Mr Monkey couldn't believe his ears. Imagine Pa Alligator, with all his airs, asking who is trouble!

Mr Monkey grinned mischievously. 'You want to see trouble, Pa Alligator?'

'Sure enough.' Pa Alligator raised his snout.

'I had better not bother. You are not going to like trouble!' Mr Monkey could hardly keep a straight face.

'But I tell you, I want to see trouble!' Pa Alligator couldn't bear to think that Mr Monkey knew more than he did. After all, he was better than those land creatures.

Mr Monkey scratched his head and picked some fuzz from his legs. 'Okay, okay. Meet me here 'bout ten o'clock tomorrow and I'll take you to see trouble.'

With that, Mr Monkey scampered off, laughing to himself.

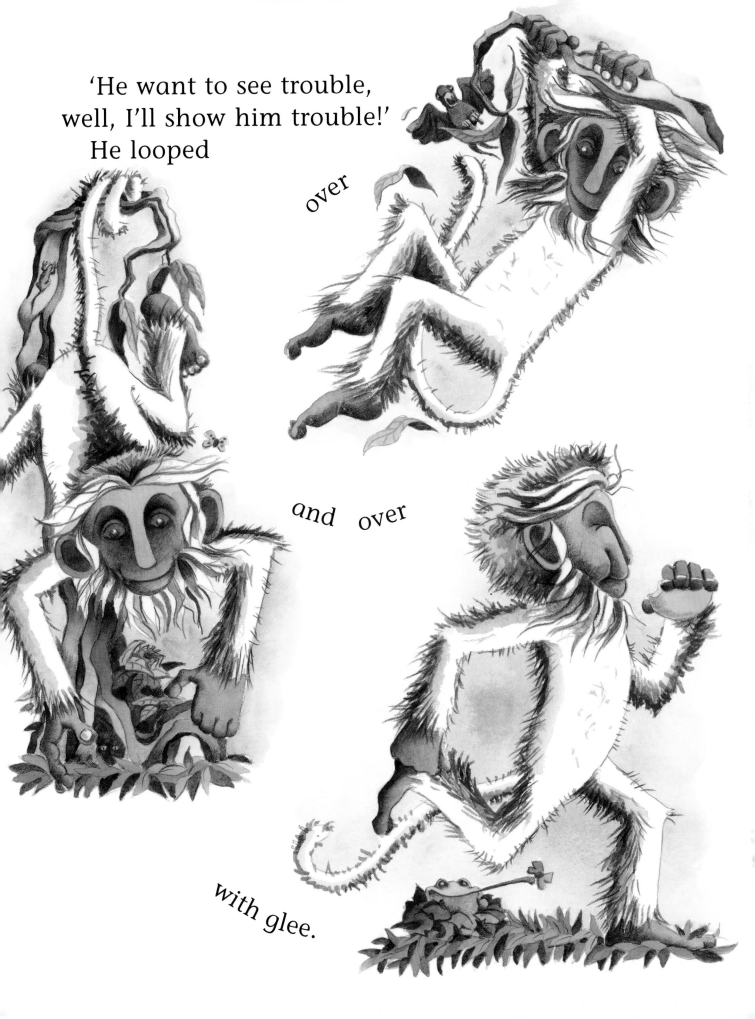

'He want to see trouble,
well, I'll show him trouble!'
He looped

over

and over

with glee.

That night, Mr Monkey called his wife and twelve children and told them exactly what he wanted them to do.

At five o'clock the next morning, Ma Monkey and her twelve children scampered to the hill near to Papa Joe's house. Ma Monkey lined her twelve children up from the bottom of the hill to the top of the hill.

Ma Monkey filled buckets with water from the well by Papa Joe's house.

Up the hill the buckets went then down the water came.

16

From the bottom of the hill to the top

it went over and over again.

They threw water down the path on the
opposite side of the hill too.
    They passed the buckets up,
          they passed the buckets down.
From the top of the hill the water spilled
          over and over again.

Ma Monkey filled one hundred buckets of water. The ground was muddy and slippery.

That morning, Pa Alligator began to get ready.

He ate small fish and crayfish and bugs and frogs.

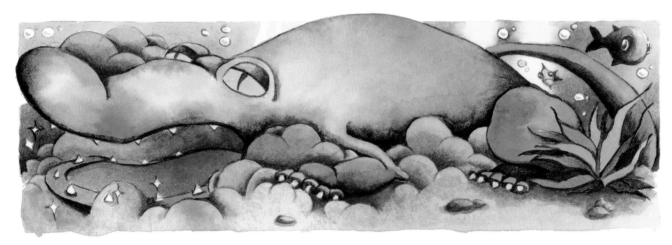

He shined his sharp teeth on the sand on the bottom of the river.

He swished his tail from left to right to get rid of the mud on his skin.

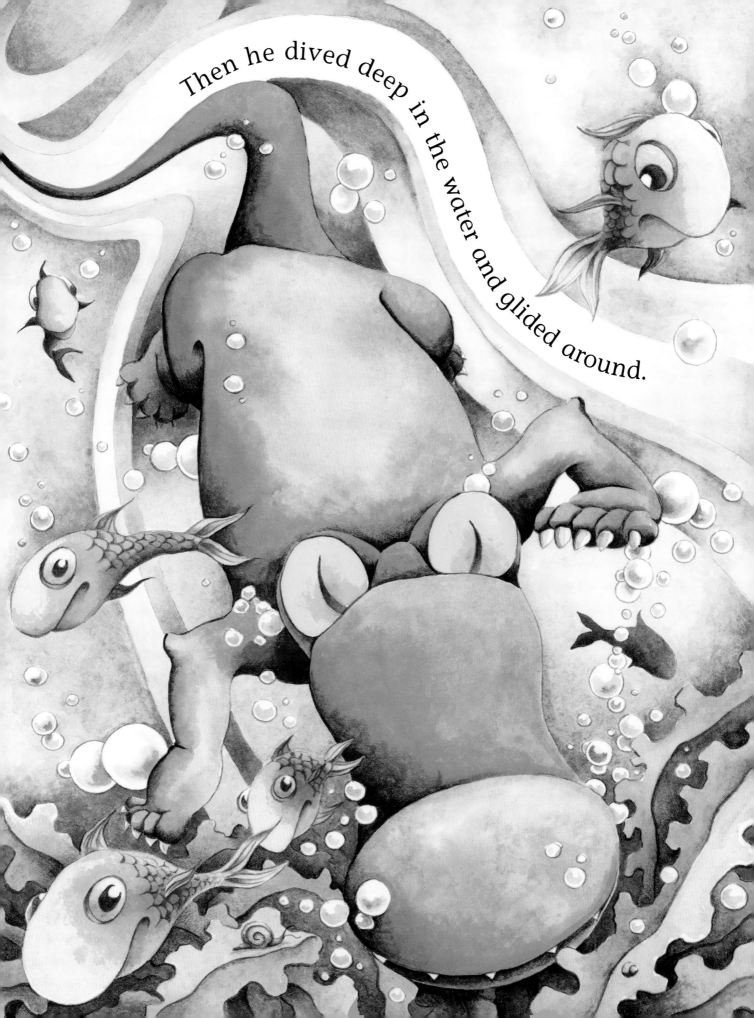

Then he dived deep in the water and glided around.

Ma Alligator watched him. 'Where are you going, Pa?'

Pa Alligator pretended that he didn't hear her, but she asked again and again. Finally, Pa Alligator said, 'I'm going to see trouble with Mr Monkey.'

Well, Ma Alligator had never seen trouble either so she begged Pa Alligator to take her. Their six children woke up and they wanted to see trouble too.

They all ate small fish and crayfish and bugs and frogs. They shined their sharp teeth on the sand on the bottom of the river. They swished their tails to get rid of the mud on their skins. They dived deep and came up shiny and clean.

Pa Alligator and his family crawled out onto the river bank to wait for Mr Monkey.

At ten o'clock, Mr Monkey came looping up.
'Morning, Pa Alligator. I see you brought your
whole family,' he said.

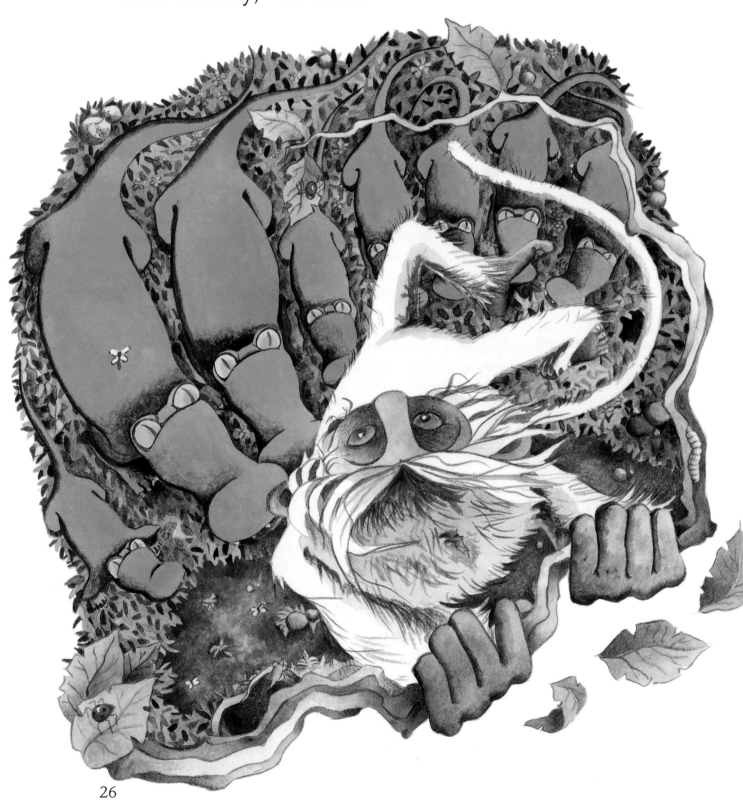

Pa Alligator crawled closer to Mr Monkey and whispered. 'I hope you don't mind, but they wanted to see trouble too.'

'Mind? Oh no, Pa Alligator, look how nice and clean they're looking! Bring them too.' Mr Monkey scratched his head. He could hardly keep a straight face.

Mr Monkey led them past the big mango tree, into the bushes. He led them straight to Papa Joe's house.

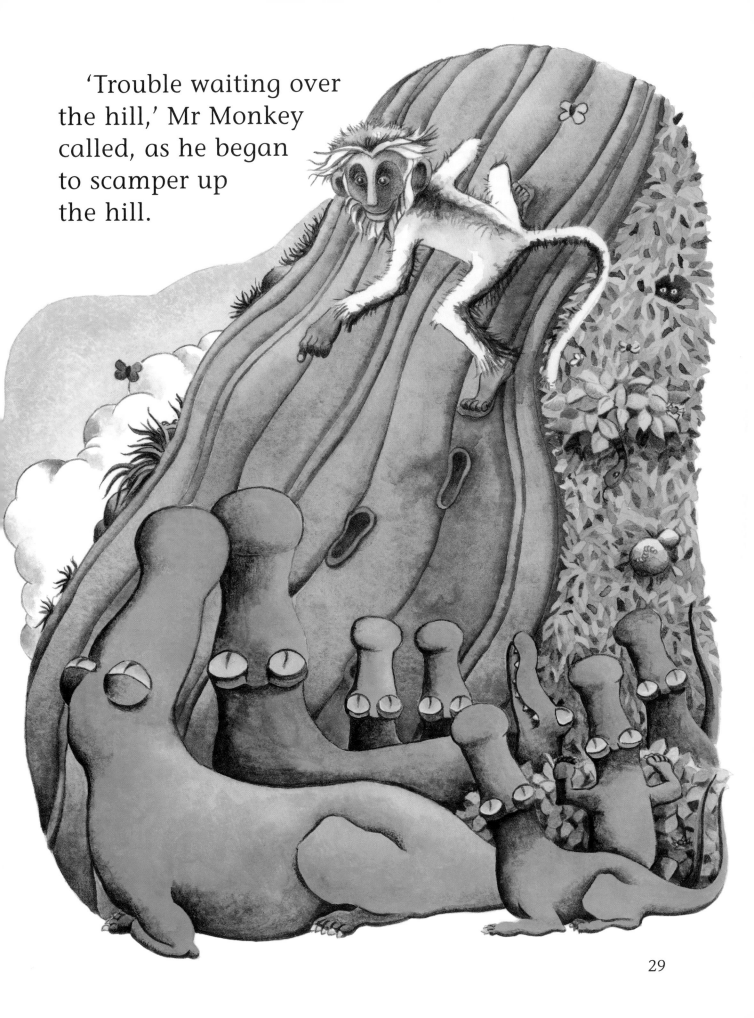

'Trouble waiting over the hill,' Mr Monkey called, as he began to scamper up the hill.

Pa Alligator, Ma Alligator and their six
children
kept slipping
and sliding
back down
the hill.

They couldn't get
a firm grip
with their
feet.

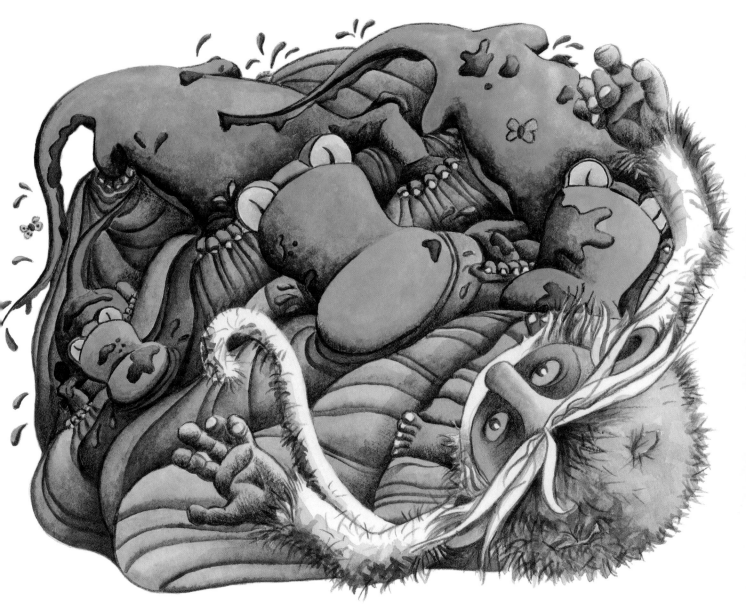

'Come on, come on, trouble waiting over the hill!' Mr Monkey shouted. He had already reached the top of the hill.

'Where are we going?' Ma Alligator asked. She was getting anxious. They had never been so far from the river.

'Not far now, not far now,' Mr Monkey grinned, as he disappeared over the hill.

At the top of the hill, Pa Alligator, Ma Alligator and their six children stood and stared.

Near the bottom of the hill, water stretched as far as they could see. The water was bluer than the sky.

'Wha . . . wha . . . what's that, Pa?' Ma Alligator asked. But Pa Alligator didn't know.

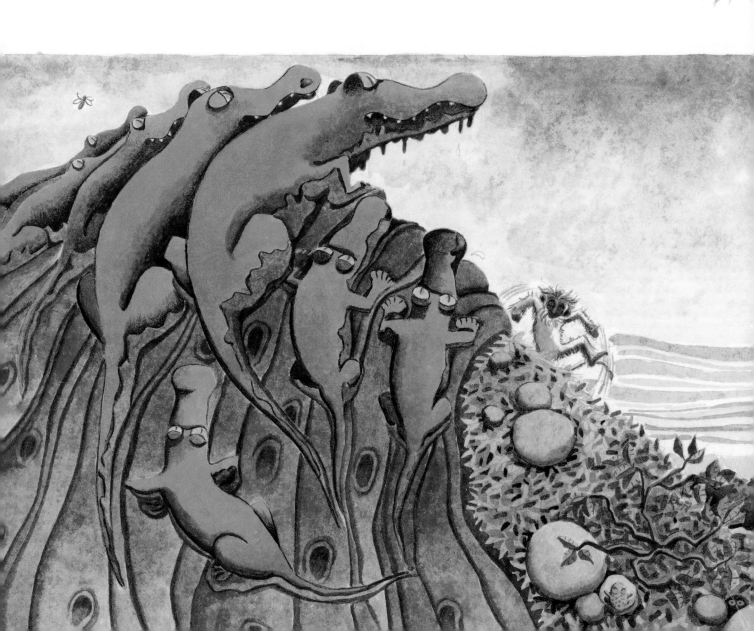

Just then, Mr Monkey came looping back.
'What you stopping for?' he asked.
Pa Alligator, Ma Alligator and their six
children just stood and stared.

Mr Monkey scratched his head and watched them. 'You never seen the sea?'

Pa Alligator didn't answer. After all, he was smarter than those land creatures. How could he tell Mr Monkey that he had never seen the sea?

Pa Alligator and his family kept staring at the sea. And then Pa Alligator slipped.

He skidded and skated on the sloshy, slippery slope. Ma Alligator tried to hold his tail. But she skidded and skated and slipped on the soggy, squashy slope too.

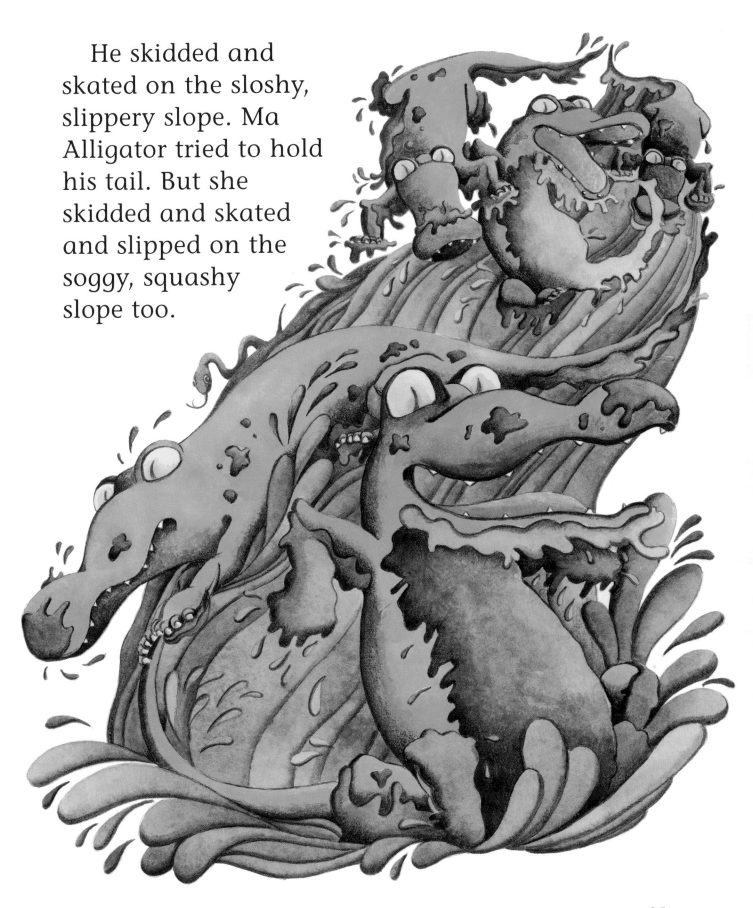

Their six children came careening down behind them. They could not stop.

They tumbled and turned.
They wriggled and wiggled.
They bawled
and called
as they rolled over
and over
down
the sloshy,
slippery
slope.

Mr Monkey watched them. He screeched and chattered and danced and pranced. 'You see trouble, Pa Alligator? This is trouble!' he shouted.

Just then, Mr Monkey slipped. He started to slide down the slippery, slimy slope. He jumped onto Pa Alligator's back and held on tight.

They all slithered and slid down the sloshy, soggy, slope. Finally they tumbled onto a pile of stones at the bottom of the hill.

Pa Alligator and his family had bruises and lumps and mud all over their shiny clean skin. They wanted to go back home immediately.

Mr Monkey screeched and somersaulted. He sat picking mud from his hands and legs.

'You see what trouble is, Pa Alligator? Next time, don't go asking foolishness like who is trouble!'

Pa Alligator was vexed. 'Now that Mr Monkey feels he knows more than I do!'

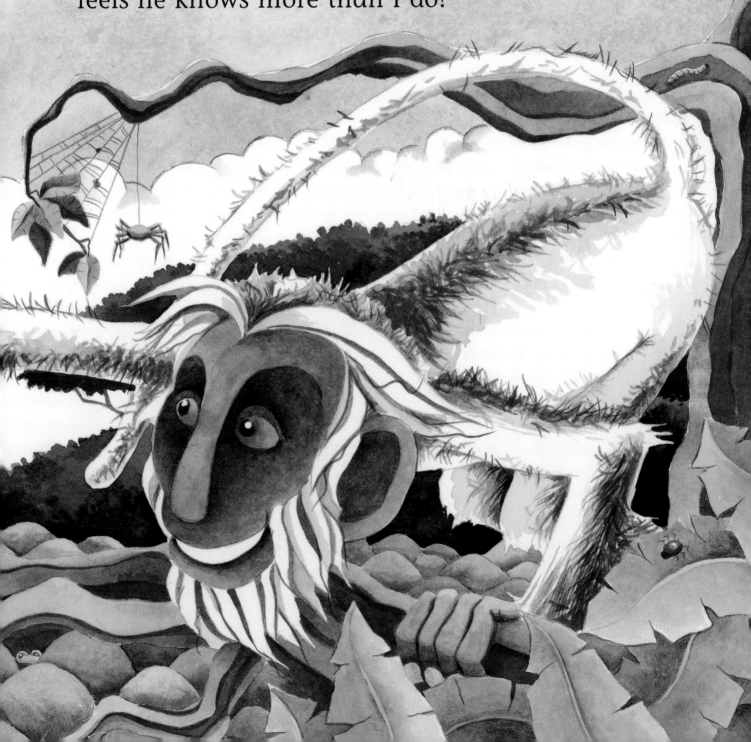

Mr Monkey scampered off to an old hut near the bottom of the hill and called his wife and twelve children.

They screeched and chattered and danced and pranced.

Mr Monkey, Ma Monkey and their twelve
children led Pa Alligator, Ma Alligator and their
six children back to the river. This time, they
passed where the earth was dry and hard.
They passed Papa Joe's house
and crawled through the bushes.
They passed under the big mango tree,
back to the river.

Pa Alligator and his family slithered quickly
into the water, without a word to Mr Monkey.
Pa Alligator, Ma Alligator and their six
children soaked in the water.

The next morning, when they came up to sun themselves on the river bank, their skin was hard. They were blue and black and lumpy where they had bruised themselves, tumbling down that sloshy, slimy, slippery slope.

Their skin has remained just like that to this day.

So now, when alligators come out of the water to lie on the river bank in the morning sun, they don't swish their tails and cock their snouts in the air. They don't close their eyes and turn away whenever land creatures pass by.

They crawl and snarl and snap and clamp and hump and chump and claw and gnaw on any land creatures that cross their path.

And monkeys still pick their fur but they keep far, far, far away from alligators!

For my darling grandsons
Jonathon and Joshua

Macmillan Education
Between Towns Road, Oxford OX4 3PP
A division of Macmillan Publishers Limited
Companies and representatives throughout the world

www.macmillan-caribbean.com

ISBN 0-333-95438-6

Text © Lynette Comissiong 2005

Illustration © Rachel Parker 2005

First published 2005

Typeset by Melissa Orrom Swan
All Illustrations by Rachel Parker

Printed and bound in Thailand

2009 2008 2007 2006 2005
10 9 8 7 6 5 4 3 2 1